Dear Parent:
Your child's love of reading starts here!

Every child learns to read in a different way and at his or her own speed. Some go back and forth between reading levels and read favorite books again and again. Others read through each level in order. You can help your young reader improve and become more confident by encouraging his or her own interests and abilities. From books your child reads with you to the first books he or she reads alone, there are I Can Read Books for every stage of reading:

SHARED READING
Basic language, word repetition, and whimsical illustrations, ideal for sharing with your emergent reader

BEGINNING READING
Short sentences, familiar words, and simple concepts for children eager to read on their own

READING WITH HELP
Engaging stories, longer sentences, and language play for developing readers

READING ALONE
Complex plots, challenging vocabulary, and high-interest topics for the independent reader

ADVANCED READING
Short paragraphs, chapters, and exciting themes for the perfect bridge to chapter books

I Can Read Books have introduced children to the joy of reading since 1957. Featuring award-winning authors and illustrators and a fabulous cast of beloved characters, I Can Read Books set the standard for beginning readers.

A lifetime of discovery begins with the magical words **"I Can Read!"**

Visit www.icanread.com for information
on enriching your child's reading experience.

I Can Read Book® is a trademark of HarperCollins Publishers.

Library of Congress catalog card number: 2011935005
ISBN 978-0-06-208606-8 (trade bdg.)—ISBN 978-0-06-208605-1 (pbk.)

14 15 16   SCP   10 9 8 7 6 5 4 3   ❖   First Edition

I Can Read!

BEGINNING 1 READING

Dixie

and the Class Treat

WITHDRAWN

story by Grace Gilman
pictures by Jacqueline Rogers

HARPER
An Imprint of HarperCollinsPublishers

Emma came home from school.

Dixie wagged her tail.

Dixie was happy to see Emma.

"I have a big project to do,"

Emma told Dixie.

Emma went to find her mom.
"Tomorrow it is my turn
to bring a snack for my class.
I want to make something special,"
said Emma.

"How about oatmeal spice cookies?"
said Emma's mom.

Emma and her mom went to the kitchen.

Emma got the flour and the eggs.

Her mom got the sugar and spices.

"Wash your hands before we start,"
said Emma's mom.

"And please don't make such a mess."

Emma's mom cracked the eggs.

Emma was about to mix in

the sugar and cinnamon

when Dixie ran back into the room.

Dixie barked. Dixie jumped.

Dixie bumped into the table . . .

. . . and knocked over everything!

"Dixie! You made a giant mess!"
Emma said.

Emma and her mom cleaned up

and started all over again.

When all the cookies were ready,

they put them in the oven.

It was almost bedtime
by the time the cookies were done.
Emma's mom helped her put
them into fancy bags for everyone.

The next day, Emma was excited as she got ready for school.

Dixie wagged her tail.

Emma left some cookies at home and took the rest to school.

After Emma left,

Dixie sniffed the food.

Dixie grabbed a bag off the counter
and ripped it open.

Just then, Emma's mom came in.

Dixie spit out the cookies she took.

"Uh-oh. If Dixie doesn't like them,

something must be wrong,"

said Emma's mom.

Emma's mom tasted a cookie.

They were very spicy!

She opened the cinnamon

and realized it wasn't cinnamon at all!

It was superhot pepper!

The spices had gotten all mixed up

when they fell.

Meanwhile, at school,

Emma's class was ready for snack time.

They had finished a hard math lesson.

The bags of snacks were on the table.

Emma's cookies looked yummy.

Just then, the door swung open.

Emma's mom came into the room.

Dixie ran in after her.

Dixie barked. Dixie leaped.

Dixie jumped on the table.

Bags of cookies flew everywhere!

"No, Dixie! Get down!"
cried Emma. But it was too late.
The room was a mess.
Her snacks were ruined.

"Dixie was trying to help,"

said Emma's mom.

"The cookies are bad."

Emma's mom told her that

the spices had gotten mixed up.

"Dixie saved the day!"

said Emma's friend Amy.

Dixie barked.

"But what about snack time?"

Emma asked.

"Don't worry," said her mom.

"I made some the right way!"

The class cheered.

They all ate the new batch of cookies.

When they were done,

the teacher said, "Let's go outside!"

They all ran to the playground.

"It's time for the relay race,"
said Emma's teacher.

"Emma, Dixie can be on your team."

All the kids ran in the race,

but Emma and Dixie won!

"Dixie deserves a treat,"

Emma told her mom.

Her mom gave her a dog treat.

Emma made it pretty.

Dixie loved it.